THE NIGHT
THE PILLOW POPPED

Hannah Jayne never went to bed
without her favorite pillow.
She pat it back and forth, back and forth,
every night until she fell asleep.

Mama always packed it for sleepovers
at Grandma and Grandpa's special igloo.
She even packed it for family vacations.

Hannah Jayne never shut her eyes
unless her special pillow was with her.

She patted it...
and patted it.

And when the Spring morning sun woke her,
she held it tight in her arms.
It made her feel warm, safe, and happy.

But then one day she saw a little hole in it.
She wondered how it got there and asked Mama
to please fix the pillow's boo-boo.

Mama hugged her and said she would make it all better
with her magical needle and thread.
By bedtime, the pillow was as good as new,
and Hannah Jayne slept like an angel through
the warm Summer nights.

But later on that year,
the sun began to set in the sky earlier each night
and Mama explained that Autumn was here.

Through the window, Hannah Jayne noticed
the green leaves on the big oak tree turn bright yellow,
orange, and fire-engine red.
The colorful leaves even danced as they fell to the ground
and created a crisp blanket of confetti.

Hannah Jayne knew Winter was around
the corner and that is when
she saw more and more holes in her pillow—
maybe even too many for Mama to fix.

Holes and all, Hannah Jayne still loved her pillow!
But that night when she jumped into bed
she hugged her pillow so tightly that...

IT POPPED!

POOF!
Feathers went everywhere.

She cried. This time a magical needle
and thread could not fix the pillow,
so Mama came into Hannah Jayne's bedroom instead
and hugged her until she fell asleep.

It was the very first night Hannah Jayne
slept without her special pillow.

The sun shined brighter than ever that morning
and when Hannah Jayne woke up without
her special pillow, she smiled and knew.
She knew Mama was right.

She could sleep without
her favorite pillow. Hannah Jayne did it!

And that was the night the pillow popped.